CW00553953

The Adventures

of

Jemima

and

Edward Jackson

Book 1

Jeff Woodbridge

Illustrated by Michael Welsh

ISBN: 9798370555046

PublishNation
www.publishnation.co.uk

The Jemima series of books
are dedicated to my granddaughters
Emily and Olivia Woodbridge.
Without whose constant requests
for a story at bedtime,
they might never have been written.

Chapter 1

Edward Jackson was 10 years old.

'I'm nearly 11, and I don't need a babysitter,' he shouted, stamping his foot and accidentally breaking one of the toys he had been playing with and left lying on the floor. This promptly made him hop around holding his foot in his hand.

Jemima closed her eyes, shook her head and sighed.

'You're 10, and you had a birthday just a few weeks ago,' said his sister, walking away from the living room of the house their parents owned, 'and mum said you have to do as I say.'

Mum and dad were at work and for the first week of the school holidays, Jemima had been told to stay in, finish her homework, (which she hadn't started), and supervise her brother.

Edward sulked, hopping after his sister, 'I want to go out and play', he said more to the room than to Jemima, who was already climbing the stairs and heading to tidy her bedroom.

'You can go and have your breakfast and keep out of my way,' she shouted, without turning to see if he was there.

He was there.

He was always there.

He followed her around like sheep in a field. Jemima thought of herself as grown up now that she was a teenager.

'You know I can't reach the cereal off the top shelf and anyway, I want to stay with you.'

Jemima puffed out a big sigh, raised her eyes to the ceiling and turned around, just in time to see him pick up her new bedside clock.

'And you can leave that alone, it's mine!' she shouted loud enough to make him almost drop it.

He carefully put it down and moved away from the bed.

'I was only looking,' he said moodily, trying to put both his feet into one of her slippers.

The clock had been a birthday gift from her nan and grandad. Odd, really, because they usually bought clothes for her and toys for Edward.

She sat on the side of her bed and picked it up.

'You had better not have broken it, it's still quite new.'

He came and sat beside her, squashing her space and making her move sideways.

'It's ugly, why did they buy that for you? And look at that stupid thing on the front.'

He had a point. The face of the clock had a design that started at the bottom and looked like 3D flower stems climbing up either side of the dial and joining up again over the top. There was something not quite right about the face, but she couldn't put her finger on what it was. She put the clock down.

'Come on, let's go down and I'll get your breakfast cereal,' she said, standing up and heading towards the stairs, thinking forward to the time when he would be tall enough to do it for himself.

Jemima was an average height, average weight, average looking type of girl with long, red hair forever tied back in a ponytail. She had the beginnings of beauty starting to shine when she smiled.

She didn't smile however, when she had to look after her temperamental little brother and she resented this obligation.

Edward, on the other hand, was small for his age with blonde hair that did whatever it wanted, no matter how it was cut or combed. He was naturally clumsy as if he was still growing into his skin, which of course he was.

He absolutely adored his big sister. He wanted to be around her, play with her things and generally interact with her whenever he could despite the 3-year difference in their ages.

Jemima, however, thought him babyish, needy, and much too young to be classed as a friend. She loved him, of course she did, but she didn't want him continually in her face. Needless to say, things didn't always work out well.

'And when you've finished that,' she said with a grin that could easily have been mistaken for a scowl, 'you can go wash your face, clean your teeth, and get yourself dressed. I have homework to do.'

Chapter 2

Edward ate his breakfast alone, as his sister stomped off back to her room. 'I want to go and do something,' he complained quietly to himself.

He left the half-finished cereal bowl and the empty glass of orange juice that Jemima had poured for him, on the table and did as his sister said. It didn't even occur to him to put them in the sink.

He went up to his bedroom.

'Why is my room always such a mess?' he thought to himself, as he dropped his PJ's onto the floor, covering some toy cars he had been playing with last week and dressed himself in the same clothes he had been wearing since the weekend.

He was bored and managed to break several toy animals by throwing them around, pretending they could fly.

In the end, he wandered down the hall to his sister's room, opened the door and walked in without knocking.

Jemima shouted at him, 'What do you want? I didn't hear you coming, you scared me half to death.'

'I'm bored, can we go outside?'

'No,' she snapped, 'mum said you weren't allowed out since you broke her favourite cup yesterday and anyway, I still have stuff to do.'

'But I want to play,' he whined, sitting on her bed and picking up her clock again. 'Can I look at this?'

She looked at him. 'No, leave it alone, you'll only break it.'

She turned back to her desk and picked up her pen, 'I have to finish this homework before dad gets home.'

Edward slid down onto the floor, with his back against her bed, facing away from his sister, and was turning the clock around in his little hands.

'That's a strange thing,' he said to himself, looking at the centre of the clock where the hands join, 'there's a picture in the middle.'

He heard his sister sigh again but he didn't look up. 'Do you have a magnifying glass?'

'I told you to put that down,' she yelled at him from her desk, 'if you break it, I'll have to tell mum and then explain it to grandad.'

'No, I mean it, there is a little picture here and it looks like an old castle.' He was squinting at the centre of the clock.

She picked her head up off her arms. Her pen bounced onto the floor.

'Oh, for Gods' sake,' she huffed, but slouched over towards him, 'how am I ever going to get some work done when you keep interrupting?'

'You need to see what's here, and this plant thing came loose on its own... I didn't do it, honest.'

'Oh Jesus... do you have to ruin everything you touch?' she said as she sat on the floor beside him.

'Look, here,' and he pointed to where she should be looking.

Jemima took the clock off him and was touching the loose strand that had come adrift on the clockface.

'It's soft. I'm sure it wasn't like that before.'

'No, here,' he said, again, trying to attract her attention to his discovery and pointing to the middle.

'Wait, I'm looking at this bit first.'

The strand seemed to waft and wave as she stroked it and as she did, the picture in the centre seemed to grow. And grow.

Suddenly and without warning, the two children were sucked into the picture with a loud 'Whooosh!'

Chapter 3

They landed rather uncomfortably on straw, in what could only be described as the inside of a dungeon. The room was cold, and the light was dim.

Edward whimpered and held on to his sister. 'Jemima, what just happened?'

'I told you not to keep playing with my clock,' she said, accusingly.

'And I told you there was a picture in it but you wouldn't listen,' he responded, also accusingly.

There were bars made of iron on three sides, and a damp, dark stone wall with iron rings set in, behind them. In one of the sides there was a door, also made of iron bars, and it was ajar.

Jemima untangled herself from Edward and stood up. She staggered towards the door as best she could with her snivelling brother still hanging on tight to her leg.

'Edward, let go, I can't walk unless you do. Here, hold my hand.'

Reluctantly he released her, stood up and gripped her hand instead.

'Don't leave me, I'm scared.'

Jemima looked at him and sighed.

'I won't, now let's get out of here.'

They moved silently forward, Jemima leading, one hand on the bars, the other having its life squeezed out.

They went through the door and continued to the end of the room. Jemima stopped. She stuck her head out to find they were in a corridor. They could go left or right.

'Which way is right?' she asked herself aloud.

'I want to go home,' squeaked a voice behind her.

Ignoring her brother, she listened. There were voices in the distance to her right, and there was a bright light in the distance to her left.

She chose to go left. It was lit with wall lights at high level and although several didn't work, she could see quite clearly.

Keeping close to the stone wall, they moved forward. There was another row of cells opposite her, each the same as the one they had just come from. The doors were open and there was no-one around.

As they approached a corner, Jemima had to remind her brother to keep quiet. His grizzling was going to be heard sooner or later.

'I can't help it, I want to go home.'

'Well shush as much as you can,'

She stopped and took a quick peep around the corner. They were at another corridor. It was better lit and had stone walls on both sides. She chose to go left again. If nothing else, she'd be able to find her way back by taking right turns, not that she wanted to come back this way.

Again, staying close to one wall, they tiptoed their way towards a much brighter area.

As they approached another corner, there was a heavy wooden door, and it was open.

She unpeeled her hand from Edward, told him not to move and inched her way inside the room.

Chapter 4

It was empty of people although there was an old, grey motheaten sofa with motheaten cushions on it in the centre of the room.

She went to turn around and crashed straight into her brother who had followed her and now clung onto her arm.

'Edward,' she whispered loudly, 'I told you to wait outside.'

He just whimpered.

She sighed.

He gripped her hand tightly as they moved slowly around the walls, then stopped. The hair on the back of Jemima's neck stood up. She felt as if they were being watched.

And indeed, they were.

On the cushions of the old, grey motheaten sofa were a pair old, grey eyes.

Jemima stared at the eyes.

The eyes stared at them.

Edward started to cry. 'What are they? What do they want?'

'Shush.'

The eyes continued to stare.

Jemima didn't take her eyes off of them either.

Then the eyes started to lift, and a huge mouth gaped open into a huge yawn. Another pair of old eyes appeared from further down the old sofa. They too yawned but were much smaller than the first.

'And who might you be?' asked the larger eyes.

Jemima stared. Edward whimpered.

'Who are you and where are we?' Jemima asked quietly, completely ignoring the question and much too frightened to wonder that the eyes had spoken.

The eyes now raised up into a long stretch. First forward, then back and revealed themselves to belong to a very old, greying Red Setter dog that now moved off the sofa and walked slowly towards them.

Edward whimpered and hid behind his sister.

'So, who might you be?' it repeated as it sat in front of her, their heads at the same level.

'I'm Jemima and this is my brother Edward.'

'And why are you here?'

'Where is here? I don't know where we are.'

'You don't know where you are? Well, how did you get in?'

Jemima looked at the old dog. Edward whimpered from behind her even more.

'I had a magic clock and we fell into it.'

Chapter 5

She tried to make it sound less silly but only succeeded in feeling more foolish.

'We didn't mean to come here, wherever here is.'

'Ah, I wondered where that clock had gone. You are in the Castle Bloodstock, and we are the Guardians of the Dungeons. I am the Major but we haven't had many prisoners to look after since the new master took over many years ago.'

'How can we get back then, I still have homework to finish, and Dad'll go mad if we're not there when he gets home.'

'You will need to make your way to the upper levels but don't worry, time doesn't go as fast here as in the outside world.'

Jemima looked at the Major. The Major looked at her.

'If you follow this corridor, it will take you to a staircase. You will need to go up the stairs to find your way out. Do not go down. There is nothing but trouble below this level. Good luck.'

With that, the Major turned and slowly strolled back. He climbed carefully onto the old grey sofa and closed his eyes. The smaller eyes closed too, and the sound of soft snoring soon filled the room.

Edward, who had finally stopped snivelling, took his sisters hand again.

'Can we go home now?'

'We have to find the stairs,' she told him as they set off in the direction the Major had suggested.

They walked quickly and when the stairs appeared, Jemima stopped. She looked down into the darkness and wondered what was so terrible down there.

'No, we have to go up,' said Edward, pulling her in the other direction, 'the dog said to go up.'

Jemima looked at him.

'What? Yes, of course,' she said distractedly and started heading up the stairs.

There were no handrails and it took Edward longer to climb than Jemima, but eventually they came to a landing. There was a choice of two directions.

Chapter 6

Jemima chose the small one. It was covered in soil and tree bark and opened into a little cavern. They appeared to have arrived in the root system of a gigantic tree. The walls were made of dirt and roots littered the floor but there was light coming from inside.

Jemima automatically headed that way. There were several tunnels leading away and she stopped to decide which one to follow.

'Who are you?' said an echoey voice, that made Jemima jump. Edward whimpered.

'Who said that?' she whispered, her voice seemed loud in the quiet of the cavern.

'Who are YOU?' the voice repeated.

'I'm Jemima and this is my brother Edward,' she said trying to locate the sound.

A head poked out from a tunnel to her right.

'What do you want here?' said the head, grumpily.

'We're looking for the way home, the Major said it was up the stairs.'

'Yes, it is, but you should have taken the other direction.'

'Oh, I'm sorry, we'll go.'

She turned to leave and walked straight into Edward, who had hidden himself behind her again and they both fell over.

The voice waited until they had picked themselves up.

'Before you go, will you do something for me?'

Jemima watched as a large red squirrel came out from the tunnel and stood in front of her. Edward hid behind her.

'My name is Samson, and my wife has something in her foot, can you help her?'

As he spoke, another large red squirrel appeared from a different tunnel and limped across towards them.

'Ah, this is my wife, and she isn't very happy.'

Jemima stepped back as Mrs Squirrel went nose to nose with her. She was about to turn and run when a smile appeared on the squirrels' face.

'Please, if you will just take a look?' she said and staggered back down one of the tunnels.

Jemima hesitated, smiled, and shrugged her shoulders.

'Of course. Why not? I'm a nurse now, but I don't do miracles on a Thursday.' she said to herself sarcastically but followed the squirrel anyway.

She found her laid on a dirt bed with her injured foot resting on a mound of earth.

Jemima only needed one look. There was a large rose thorn sticking out between the pads of her foot. She gripped it firmly with both hands and bracing herself against the dirt bed, pulled as hard as she could.

Jemima fell backwards and landed on her back on the floor, as Mrs Squirrel screamed.

Samson came running in with a worried look on his face.

Jemima beamed and held up a hand. Between her finger and thumb was the biggest, sharpest thorn she had ever seen in her life.

'Oh, Thank you, thank you.'

Jemima just smiled. Mrs Squirrel sat on the edge of her dirt bed and rubbed her foot.

'That feels so much better. Thank you indeed.'

Jemima sat up.

'We need to get moving, we have more stairs to climb. Tell me, what is below the dungeon that we're not to go near?'

The squirrels stopped what they were doing and looked at each other.

'Please say you won't go near that terrible place. Down there is the most awful creature that ever lived. It rarely comes up here but when it does, everyone hides in the hope it doesn't find them.'

Jemima gasped.

What sort of creature could make the squirrels' that frightened of it?

'Of course,' she said, with a worried look on her face, 'does it come up often?'

'Not recently, but it pays to stay on your guard.'

Jemima and Edward walked back to the staircase and started to climb again.

'Do you think the monster will come and get us?' he said nervously, 'I want to go home.'

'No, Samson said it hasn't been seen recently.'

'But that means it's due to visit?'

'Edward, stop thinking about it and get in front of me up these stairs.' Jemima said quietly, pushing him forward, but she looked quickly over her shoulder just in case.

Chapter 7

As they reached the next landing, Jemima saw more options, more directions.

She decided to take the left one. It was a wooden spiral staircase set against the stone walls and had a greasy, thick rope as a handrail.

As they started to climb, their feet made a loud stamping noise on the wooden treads. Jemima stopped. She took off her shoes and told Edward to do the same.

He griped and moaned, 'I don't want to, my feet will get cold.'

She glared at him. He took off his shoes.

Jemima looked at his socks, then at his face. Edward looked at his socks and the big toes sticking out through both of them, then looked back at Jemima.

'What? They were alright yesterday.'

Jemima sighed.

'We need to be quiet. We don't know what's up there.'

As they reached the top, she could hear a lot of banging and shouting coming from behind one of the two doors ahead.

She listened with an ear to the door, when the other door went CRASH, as it smashed into the wall beside her and bounced back. A lad of no more than fifteen years old came marching through and straight down the spiral stairs without noticing them.

Edward whimpered and Jemima put a finger to her lips to suggest that he made no more noise.

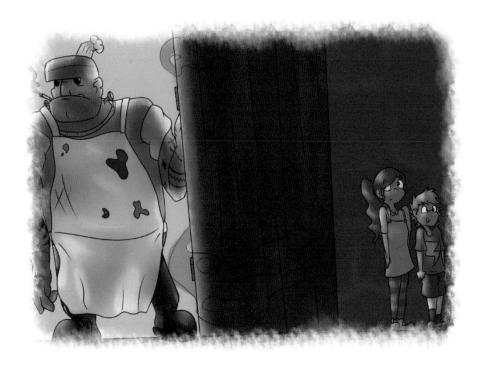

On her knees, she looked around the edge
of the door to see a kitchen, with lots of
steaming pans on a long cooker and a very
large man with his shirt sleeves rolled up to
his stained grey apron. Tattoos covered his
arms. He had a large, dirty white hat on his
bald head and a half-smoked cigarette
sticking out of his mouth. There were

stitches across his wrists and a bolt stuck out either side of his neck.

Jemima quickly pulled her head back as the man shuffled towards the door.

'An' 'urry up wiv' those veggies too,' he hollered at the staircase and slammed the door shut. The distant sound of feet returning upstairs made Jemima look around for somewhere to hide. She settled on a small, hatched door, a couple of feet off the floor, set in the wall next to where she stood.

She opened the hatch. 'Edward, get IN,' she said, pushing her brother through. She could hear him shouting as he disappeared down the tube, and she jumped in herself, hearing the hatch close as the footsteps neared the top of the stairs.

The tube went round a couple of times before expelling them into a smelly, greasy cauldron, half full of potato peelings and rotting waste vegetable matter.

Jemima climbed out and helped Edward out, just as a bucketful of vegetable offcuts came flying from the tube into the vat they had just vacated.

'Cor, you stink,' said Edward, catching a noseful of Jemima.

'Yeah well, you're not too clever yourself,' she replied, 'but I think we'd better get out of here now, before someone comes in.'

She looked around and saw a few sacks that contained veggie matter stacked against a wall. Next to them was a door. Feet slopping, they walked across the room.

Chapter 8

As they approached, Jemima stopped and listened. She could hear low murmured voices, so she quietly opened the door a fraction and peered out.

The voices were coming from the left, so still tiptoeing, she led Edward off to the right. It was a short corridor and led to another door. This one had a window in it and she could see a staircase. Silently they crept out and started to climb these stairs.

It wasn't until they were half way up that she noticed Edward didn't have his shoes. She'd been carrying hers, but he had lost his in the vat.

It was too late to go back so they continued up to the next landing. There they found a bedroom of sorts. Dust and cobwebs were everywhere.

There was an old, dirty bedspread, wrinkled and half draped on the floor. Two pillows without covers, were stained brown and were lying at angles on top of it. There were dirty, used clothes scattered all over the floor.

Edward picked up a shirt that although wasn't clean, didn't smell too badly. Quick as a flash he had whipped off his stinking jumper and replaced it with the shirt. He chose some grubby jogging bottoms and put them on too.

Jemima found a sweatshirt that was a couple of sizes too big and smelled of BO, but that was preferable to veg peelings and pulled it on. She rolled the sleeves back several times, so it wasn't so baggy.

Edward looked in a cupboard and picked out a pair of odd shoes, one black and one brown, that fitted. Both were heavily worn and had no laces but were better than nothing.

Jemima looked out through a dirty window. The room they were in was quite a way above the ground and looked out over a narrow road, which led to the mountains in front of her. The window wouldn't budge when she tried to open it, so that wasn't going to be the way out.

Dressed in their less dirty clothes, they left through a door at the far end of the bedroom and headed down a stone staircase.

At the bottom was a landing. Jemima decided that to reach ground level, they would need to go down at least one more flight.

There were two sets of stairs, both leading down but going in different directions. Which one should she choose?

Chapter 9

Jemima heard voices coming from the right and thought she saw flashing lights.

At the dark entrance to the left staircase, she could see only spiders' webs. Large, long ones that stretched from wall to wall. Some had big spiders in the centre. This staircase hadn't been used in a long time. She didn't want to know what might be down there.

She decided to go to the right.

'Come on Edward, this looks like our best option.'

'Jemima, I'm tired and hungry and I want to go home.'

'Well, if this leads us to the front door, we'll be home in no time,' she said, although truthfully she didn't know how they were going to get home.

They started down the stairs. There were no handrails so they kept one hand on the wall as they walked. They kept going further and further down. Jemima was starting to have doubts as the wall became damp to her touch.

The sound of sparks and the flashes of coloured lights began to appear as they descended until finally, the staircase curved away to the left revealing what looked like a well-lit, high ceilinged, electrical sub-station with tubes and wires leading everywhere.

Pipes came out of the walls and led to a couple of beds. There were huge circular phials that looked like they had come from a giant chemistry set, hanging from the ceiling and cables that stretched across the room from one wall to another. Lights, in several shades of orange and red lit up the room like Wembley.

On one side against a wall, a man was hunched over a workbench, tipping a liquid from one container into another and steam was pouring from it. Jemima didn't think he was making a cup of tea.

As she and Edward reached the bottom and stepped off, an iron grille crashed down behind them and barred the way back. The man looked up, only it wasn't a man.

Chapter 10

The creature had the body of a giant but beneath his large white lab coat hung a scaly reptilian tail which swished harder as his mood changed.

He turned towards them, and Edward screamed with shock.

His large head was covered in long, thin, grey hair, but his eyebrows had gone. The eyes were different colours and one of his ears was missing.

The creature held his massive hands out in front of him and beckoned them forward. Jemima realised they had gone below the dungeon and that meant they were in trouble. She had to find another way up.

She scanned the room and spotted some steps on the other side but getting there was a different matter.

'Hello, my dearsh I heard we had vishitorsh,' the voice lisped slowly through a mouth with very few teeth, 'pleashe do come forward. I'm sho happy to shee you,'

He sounded to Jemima like a drunken Scotsman, not that she knew any Scotsmen, drunken or otherwise.

'Welcome to my laboratory. My name ish Count Igor Bloodshtock and thish ish my creation Shergeant Shwill, come and lie down on thish bed, you musht be tired after your day in my cashtle.'

From behind a wall came the shouty man from the kitchen. He wasn't as tall as the Count, and his movements were slow and deliberate.

Jemima almost laughed. It looked to her like the baddie from a really cheap film she had once seen. Only he was taller and he held a heavy, thick rolling pin in his hand. He still had his dirty kitchen apron on.

As Swill limped across at ultra-slow speed, Jemima told Edward to circle round and see if the steps she had seen led upstairs and if they did, try and find the lad from the kitchen to help them.

Keeping one eye on Swill, Jemima cautiously walked towards the Count.

'What do you want from me? I'm only looking for my way home'

'You should not have come at all, young lady. You will not be allowed to leave, now you have sheen everything here.'

'But I haven't sheen anything, sorry, seen anything. It's an old castle with old people and animals, that's all.'

'But you have, you shee. Everyone and everything in thish cashtle died hundredsh of yearsh ago and thish lab ish the only way to keep them alive. We need new bloodshtock all the time, that'sh where the cashtle getsh itsh name.'

Jemima was suddenly in a bear hug from behind as the creature grabbed her and held her firmly.

Chapter 11

She had forgotten about him while she was talking to the Count.

With no effort at all, Sergeant Swill lifted her off the ground and carried her over to a bed. No matter how much she kicked and struggled, she could not break his grip.

'Hold her on thish bed Sharge, while I get the shtrapsh tight.'

The Count cackled but with straps across her chest, waist, thighs and ankles, Jemima could not move.

She could not prevent them from putting a mask over her mouth either, and as they set up their procedure for draining her blood, she started to feel very light-headed.

She had seen Edward reach the steps but heard nothing more.

Edward, meanwhile, had run up the stairs as best he could with no laces to keep his odd shoes on and reached the dungeon. He found the Major and told him what was happening.

The Major sent his associate to find the boy, Rufus, upstairs while he accompanied Edward back down to the lab.

They'd had to watch from the bottom of the stairs as Swill grabbed Jemima and forced her onto the gurney.

'We must wait for Rufus,' said the Major, 'he hates that animal more than anything.'

They watched as the Count set up his gear and put a mask over Jemima's face.

Rufus appeared beside them, breathless. He had bruises all over his face and one of his eyes was almost closed. Samson was sitting on his shoulder.

'I'll deal with this,' he said through his cut lips, and picked up a large handful of dirt and dust from the floor.

He made out to stagger across the room towards the bed and dragged a foot as he went.

The scientist turned and saw him coming.

'Sharge, would you mind dealing with that?' and nodded towards the lad.

Swill looked up and smiled a toothless smile. He held his rolling pin up and waved it at Rufus.

Chapter 12

Rufus continued his stagger until he got closer and when he was within range, he threw the handful of dirt and dust up into the eyes of the beast.

As he did so, Samson leapt from Rufus' shoulder onto Swill's head. He bit the beasts' ear and dug his little claws into his cheeks.

Sergeant Swill let out a loud grunt and put both hands up to his eyes, forgetting that he was still holding the rolling pin. It slapped his long forehead hard, which made him dizzy, and he staggered round and round in circles, which made him even dizzier.

Samson jumped clear.

Unable to see, Swill swung his weapon blind as he went round and Rufus pushed him towards the creature.

As they collided, the rolling pin smashed into the head of the Count and fell to the floor.

Igor Bloodstock vanished. He disappeared as the club hit him and completely evaporated. There was not even a trace of where he had been.

Rufus picked up the weapon and bashed the back of Sergeant Swill's knees. He buckled and as he fell Rufus hit him on the head, knocking him out totally and the beast collapsed to the floor.

Edward ran over and with Rufus' help disconnected Jemima's facemask and carried her back up the staircase to the dungeon.

It turned out that Rufus had been held prisoner for many years ever since he'd once had the clock.

He told the story of how he had been imprisoned, and how the Count had regularly taken his blood, though never enough to kill him.

As they walked back to the cell, where the clock had now reappeared, the three of them prepared to be transported back to their respective time.

Jemima had recovered and was none the worse for her experience and Edward and her said a grateful thank you and goodbye to Rufus.

They touched the loose strand on the clock.

Jemima and Edward were thrown across her bedroom floor as they re-entered their real world.

Steps on the landing outside her bedroom door alerted Jemima to her fathers' approach and a head poked around the door.

'Jemima, did you hear me? I asked if you had Edward with you.'

'Yes, dad, he's here.'

'Have you finished your homework?'

'Almost,' she replied, at which point, Edward remembered his tongue.

'We'veseenthedogsandjumpedintoadungeon and Jemimahelpedthesquirrelsandtherew eremonsters.'

His words came so quick, his brain didn't have time to organise them and none of it made any sense to their father, who promptly turned his back, muttering something about 'a vivid imagination,' before heading back down with a call of 'dinner will be half an hour.'

'Thanks dad,' Jemima called back.

She finished her homework and pushed Edward towards the door.

'Come on, you must be hungry,' she said with a smile as they went downstairs to greet their parents.

Chapter 13

A few days later, dad was driving the family down to Devon, in the south-west of England for a well-earned break.

'Are we nearly there yet?' sighed Edward for the tenth time that hour.

His dad glanced across to his mum, who was sitting in the front passenger seat, and raised his eyes to the sky. She turned to look at Edward, who was sitting directly behind his dad, and tried to placate him with a packet of crisps and a fruit drink.

'Won't be long now, darling,' she said, as she watched him stuff his face with the food and wished he could be a little more like his sister and a little less like his dad.

Jemima was fast asleep in the seat behind her mum and had been for most of the journey. She always seemed to sleep when they went out in the car, even if it was just a trip to the supermarket.

The Jackson family were on their way to a caravan park and had been up since six o'clock that morning, in order to beat the traffic on the motorway.

Edward was irritable because he had not eaten any breakfast before they left. This was because he wouldn't get out of bed when he was called, preferring to huddle under his quilt and go back to sleep.

This year his parents had managed to get the same week off work in the middle of July, so the family could take a summer break together. His mum was already doubting the wisdom of this and turned back to face the windscreen with a distinctly worried frown on her face.

They were heading south down the M5 motorway and when their turn off came into sight, Mum directed her husband to get them onto the coast road towards their destination.

After a very long while, Dad turned into a driveway that twisted and turned for a bit before opening out towards a cliff, with a magnificent view of the vast English Channel ahead of them.

He pulled up in the car park to one side of a long, white, single storey building and turned off the engine.

He looked at his wife and together they stepped out of the car. Holding hands, they headed towards the chain-link fence that protected the cliff and overlooked the beach.

A couple of clunks behind them were followed by some childish cheering and whoops of joy as both children exited the car and ran to join them.

'Wow, that didn't take long.' said Jemima, still rubbing the sleep from her eyes.

'Mum, I'm hungry,' whined Edward.

'OK, we'll go and book in and pick up the keys to the caravan then we can have something to eat.'

'Stay here and don't wander off,' Dad warned Edward, and he and Mum walked round to the front of the building and disappeared inside.

Dad was relieved to find his children were more or less in the same place when they came out of the office and walked back to the car.

'What have you been doing?' he asked Jemima, as Edward showed him the palms of two hands that were covered in a purple stain.

'We picked some blackberries. Look, there's loads on these brambles.'

Mr. Jackson looked at his wife, who just shrugged her shoulders and continued wiping some of the stain from Edwards' hands.

He sighed. 'Come on, time to find our home for the next week.'

Chapter 14

They climbed back into the car, and set off down a small road towards, what looked to Edward like a million caravans.

He and his sister were chattering excitedly to each other about what they were going to do first. All thoughts of food, temporarily forgotten.

As soon as dad pulled the car in, next to a caravan at the end of a row, the kids were out and shouting with the kind of happiness that comes at times like these, regardless of the fact that it was only eight-thirty on a Sunday morning, and that most of the other caravan occupants were still asleep.

Dad tried to hush the kids as he carried in their bags, while mum tidied away the youngsters' clothes and organized the kitchen. The children continued to squeal as they found new things to play with outside the 'van.

When everyone was a little more settled and relaxed, they strolled back towards the office, where the restaurant was serving breakfast.

After they had eaten, dad said he and mum were going to lay down and rest, and the kids could go down the beach, via the twisty path, and the sea far below.

It seemed safe enough. There were some families already paddling at the waters' edge and a rocky cliff at both ends, so they couldn't get lost.

'Come back when you're bored,' dad called, 'or hungry again,' added mum quietly, looking at Edward.

'OK,' came the reply but they were already running down the path, towards the sea.

It was almost midday when they came charging back through the 'van door.

'Mum, what's for lunch?' called Edward, as he stomped into the sitting room.

'OUT,' shouted his mother, 'your shoes are soaking, what on earth have you been doing?'

Although she guessed he'd been paddling in them.

Jemima had taken her dry shoes off at the door. 'Told you, you'd be in trouble,' she said to him, poking out her tongue.

'We've been exploring some little rock pools and there's a big one too,' he said ignoring his sister, when he came back from taking his wet shoes off.

'There were crabs and starfish and all sorts in there,' he continued, without taking a breath, 'can we take the snorkels down tomorrow, dad? Please, can we?'

Edward understood that rock pools only appeared when the tide was out, so he knew he would have to wait until then.

'I guess so,' said his dad, looking for confirmation from his wife. 'I'll put them out after breakfast.'

The next day, Jemima let Edward carry their snorkel gear down the twisty path that led to the beach and the rock-pools.

Chapter 15

She fitted his mask and breathing tube and they lay on top of the rocks with their faces below the water line, watching life go on in one of the little rock pools. Tiny crabs were busy sifting the sand for whatever morsel they could eat. Shrimps and other small animals swam and drifted to and fro through the water leaving the kids in wonder, and excited to be able to see the water life in its own environment.

On the third day, Jemima decided to check out the largest rock pool, which must have been 20 metres long and wide, and meant she could swim a little instead of just lying there. It was nearer to the cliff face than the smaller pools and the rocks which formed it were higher and bigger.

Jemima was a competent swimmer for her 13 years. Edward, however, was nervous if he went out of his depth because he didn't swim as much as splash about thinking he was moving.

Jemima was casually drifting across the surface of the water when a sudden movement near the bottom caught her attention.

She twisted to where she thought the movement had come from, but there was nothing there except some sediment that had been kicked up into the water. Something had been disturbed.

She continued to look around, but all the crabs and shrimps had gone.

Jemima swam back to the rock and climbed out, trying to work out what would have caused that.

Could it have been an octopus or an eel?

She wondered to herself. She wasn't sure she wanted to be in the same pool as either of those.

She heard rather than saw her brother scrambling over towards her, his soggy, wet shoes slapping on the rocks as he came.

'Is that very deep?' he asked, when he reached her, peering carefully over the edge of the rock Jemima was sat on.

'I can stand up at the edge,' she said, as much to discourage him from going in, as well as it only being partially true.

'There is something in here though, I nearly saw it a few minutes ago.'

'Really? How can you nearly see something? How can you know if you only nearly saw it?'

'Well, I did,' she said loudly, and added softly, 'but I didn't at the same time.'

Edward started laughing. That was the funniest thing he had ever heard. He almost lost his balance he was laughing so hard. Jemima couldn't help but join in. He had an infectious laugh, and she couldn't help but laugh with him, when she realised what she had said.

As she gasped for a breath, she did lose her balance and fell off the rock into the water. This caused Edward to laugh even harder.

Jemima went under and without her mask on, she had to keep her eyes shut and hold her breath.

As her feet reached for the bottom of the pool, she felt something touch her waist.

Panic kicked in almost immediately, and she lifted her arms to reach for the rock she'd been sat on.

A pair of hands around her waist lifted her clear and pushed her up onto the rock next to her brother.

Chapter 16

Edward had stopped laughing. He was still laid on the rock, watching. His mouth was open, his eyes were wide, as if he was going to speak but had forgotten the words.

Jemima coughed some sea water out and pulled herself clear of the water, tucking her knees and feet under her, as if to prevent them from being pulled back down.

She turned and looked at the pool but there was nothing there to see.

Edward just stared. Jemima turned to him. 'What just happened?'

Edward started to stammer. 'A... A... A... A...' but he couldn't finish. Instead, he just pointed. His hand shaking as he did so.

Jemima turned back and looked where Edward was still pointing.

There, with just her head above the water, was a young girl around Jemima's age, looking at her.

'You need to be careful in this pool,' she said, 'the water has a strong undercurrent that can drown a human.'

Jemima's mouth mimicked Edwards' and hung open.

'Who are you?' she whispered.

'My name is Whoonmerfink,' but in your language it's near enough to call me 'Daisy'.

Edward had heard this but was still trying to come to terms with Whoo.. Whon.. Wherm.. and missed the Daisy bit.

He kept saying to himself 'Whoo.. Whon.. Wherm.'

Jemima looked at Daisy

'What are you doing in here? I haven't seen you before.'

'Oh, I live near here, and I come all the time,' she answered, 'I like to play with my friends. Anyway, who are you?'

'I'm Jemima, and this is my little brother Edward, we're on holiday here. Thank you for helping me out of the pool. Would you like to come and meet our parents, we have a caravan at the top, in the park up there? We can have tea.' she added, pointing to the top of the cliff.

Daisy looked at Jemima, then down at the water, and with a dive, she submerged, turned and swimming fast, leapt up out of the water, and landed on the rocks next to her.

Again, Jemima's mouth dropped open. This was no ordinary girl. Daisy had beautiful, long, yellow hair, that hung to her waist, but below that she had no legs, just a long tail, covered in blue/green iridescent scales.

Chapter 17

'Are you a m... m... mermaid?' she stuttered, struggling to understand what she had just seen.

'Of course, I am,' Daisy answered quickly, 'do you think a human could live like this. Your people can't live in water, and I can't live long out of it.'

'M... m... mermaid!' shouted Edward, recovering his ability to speak, but still pointing.

Daisy carried on, ignoring him, 'but I can breathe in or out of water, although I have to keep my scales damp, or I will dehydrate.'

'Wow,' said Jemima, 'I've never met a real mermaid.'

'm... m.. mermaid,' mumbled Edward to himself, still unable to grasp what was in front of him.

'Do you come here every day?' asked Jemima, 'we could come again tomorrow.'

'I usually come once or twice a week to see my friends, but you need to be getting out now, the tide is coming in fast, and I have to leave.'

As she said that, a wave crashed over the rocks, almost knocking the children back into the water and they quickly climbed back down to the sand.

Jemima turned and waved to Daisy, who waved back once, then dived under the water.

Back at the caravan Edward, who had been told off for wearing his shoes in the water again, tried really hard to tell his dad about 'Whoo.. Whon.. Wherm..' but when his dad looked at Jemima for an explanation, she just shrugged her shoulders. She couldn't explain it either.

The next day when Jemima went snorkelling again, Daisy did not appear. Nor the following day. The sixth day was the day before they were due to travel home, and Jemima and Edward were at the big rock pool.

Out of the blue, Daisy suddenly appeared, scaring Jemima, and causing her to panic a little and accidently swallow a mouthful of sea water.

She stood to the side of the pool and held on to the rock, coughing and spluttering, trying to lose the taste of the salt in her mouth.

Daisy was looking at her with a huge smile on her face.

'Sorry,' she said, 'I couldn't resist that. I hope you're ok.'

Jemima looked at her and smiled. Her anger didn't last long.

'Hi Daisy, I didn't see you sneak up. You really made me jump.'

'I hoped you'd come back again,' said Daisy, 'I told my friends about you, and they wanted to see what humans' really looked like.'

'Your friends are here?' Jemima asked, looking around, 'Are they like you?'

Daisy giggled. 'No, silly. Rocky is a kleptomaniac crab and at night, when the tide is in, he crawls out to steal the flags off the sandcastles on the beach. And then there's Psycho the starfish. We call him that because he thinks he's tougher than everyone else, but he really only crawls about collecting seashells.'

Jemima stood with her mouth open as she listened to Daisy, vaguely aware of her brother laid on the rock with his snorkel mask on muttering behind her. 'Whon... Whom... she's back.'

Chapter 18

'If you take a big breath,' said Daisy, 'and dive to the bottom of this rockpool, you can meet them.'

Jemima didn't need to be asked twice. She put her face mask back on and pushed off against the rock with her feet, powering herself to the bottom.

Daisy reached out and took her hand, guiding her to the underside of a particularly large rock that formed down one side of the pool.

She didn't know what she thought she would see, but she certainly didn't expect to see a huge orange crab with one large blue claw and one smaller red one, waving a plastic Union Jack sandcastle flag at her.

Rocky had to be over a foot wide and almost as long from front to back. His eyes looked like little red balls on stalks and his tiny hands were scooping sand into his mouth so quickly, Jemima couldn't see any detail to them at all.

She turned, pushed off for the surface, took another deep breath and returned to the seabed.

The flag was still being waved to her, so she gave him a little wave back.

She felt a tug on her arm and turned to see Daisy pointing to the largest display of seashells she had ever seen. Laid on top of this pile, that was half buried beneath another large rock, was a brownish, orangish, starfish almost a foot long, with only four legs and a stump where the fifth one was still regrowing.

Again, she gave a little wave and pushed off for some more air. When she surfaced, Jemima held onto the rock, trying to make sense of what she had just seen. Daisy appeared next to her.

'I hope Rocky didn't upset you,' she said, 'only he tends to be a little over friendly at times and nips me occasionally.

'No.' said Jemima, 'I needed more air, that was why I left. I think he's lovely and his colouring is brilliant. What happened to Psycho's leg?'

'He doesn't like to talk about it, but one day he went to claim a seashell and carry it back, when the occupant of the shell, which was a large Hermit crab, decided to fight for it. Well, Psycho's not known for being intelligent, and refused to let go, so the

Hermit crab used his one, big, claw and cut his leg off.'

Jemima gasped. 'Didn't that hurt him?'

'Not much,' said Daisy, 'the limbs regularly regenerate. He was more embarrassed than anything else.'

'H.. H.. Hi,' came a timid voice from above them.

'Oh, hello Edward,' said Daisy, 'are you coming in to meet my friends?'

'Th.. Th.. There's more of you?' he stammered.

'Only Rocky and Psycho,' said Daisy,' you can check out his seashells if you like.'

Edward was torn. He desperately wanted to see the shells, after all he had collected some himself this week. But he would be under water and that meant he would be out of his depth.

'I don't know,' he said quietly, 'what if I can't breathe and drown. What's dad going to say?'

'Come on silly,' said Jemima, who had had enough of his stalling and pulled him into the water. She put his mask on and adjusted her own.

'I'll hold on to you all the time and we'll need to be quick before the tide comes in again. Take a big breath and let's go.'

Chapter 19

She pushed off the rock and dived for the seabed with Edward under her arm. She reached the rock where Rocky was still waving his flag and she pointed, so that Edward would see. His eyes flashed wide open with surprise. Then she pushed him back to the surface to get another breath.

They both turned and this time Edward pushed himself off the rock to return to the bottom. He looked again at Rocky and had to be forced to turn to see Psycho and his shells.

This time, when he resurfaced, he took a breath and dived back down again with no help at all from his sister. He could not believe how many shells there were. All sizes, shapes, and colours. But it was the quantity that took his breath way.

He grabbed another lungful of air and dived to look again at Psychos' shells. Edward was in awe of his collection and it was while he stared at the seashells, Rocky stopped waving his flag and decided to join them.

He couldn't get close enough to his friend, so he gave a quick nip to whatever was in his way and then moved forward. Unfortunately, it was Edward's bottom that had been in the way and he screamed. That meant he suddenly didn't have any air to breathe with and started to panic. Wildly.

He kicked out with his shoeless feet, accidently making contact with Psychos' pile of shells.

Psycho saw this and, in retaliation, reached out and suckered himself onto one of Edwards' legs.

Rocky meanwhile had seen Psycho's attack and went to join him, nipping and gripping Edwards' big toe.

Daisy grabbed hold of Edward's arm and pushed for the surface. She shoved him up and straight out of the water onto his tummy on the rock.

She then had to persuade Rocky to let go of Edwards' big toe and Psycho to release his suckers and drop back into the rock pool, which they did reluctantly.

Jemima appeared at the surface next to her.

'Sorry, about that,' said Daisy, 'they can be a bit boisterous.'

Edward was spluttering and coughing. He looked back at where his injuries should have been. But there was hardly a mark on his leg and his toe showed no effects either.

'Monsters, they're monsters,' shouted Edward, crying and pointing, although there was nothing left to see. He backed away as far as he could on the rock.

Jemima smiled to Daisy, 'we should go, the tide won't be far behind us, and I don't think he'll be coming in again.' She nodded her head towards Edward, and Daisy glanced over.

'I'm sorry about my friends and I hope your brother is ok.'

'Oh, don't worry about him, I'll tell mum he slipped on a rock. She's used to him being clumsy and I won't tell anyone about you either,'

Jemima hugged Daisy and pulled herself up onto the rock. They exchanged a wave and Daisy was gone. She picked up their snorkelling gear and handed it over for Edward to carry.

Jemima sighed and tried to work out what she had seen today. She turned, looked towards her brother and said, 'come on you, let's go and have tea.'

Edward, whose tears had more or less stopped, looked up, coughed again, and said, 'they tried to drown me. The monsters tried to drown me.'

'What monsters?' said Jemima, 'I haven't seen any monsters.'

'Those monsters, in the water. They tried to drown me.'

'You slipped off the rock and fell in. You can't swim and you couldn't breathe,' she said sternly. 'there are no such things as monsters.'

'But.. but.. but,' he stammered.

'No,' she said, 'NO. Look, mum's waving,' she said, trying to change the subject, 'I think it's time to go back to the caravan.' And she quickened her pace towards the twisty path, making Edward run to keep up.

It turned out to be the last day of their holiday and Jemima had to pinch herself to remember what she had seen and done, although she knew she would never forget.

Printed in Poland
by Amazon Fulfillment
Poland Sp. z o.o., Wrocław